This book is dedicated to all
the great writers and illustrators who have
inspired me to make picture books.

First published 2014 by Walker Books Ltd
87 Vauxhall Walk, London SE11 5HJ

4 6 8 10 9 7 5 3

© 2014 Brun Ltd

The right of Anthony Browne to be identified as author/illustrator of this work has been
asserted by him in accordance with the Copyright, Designs and Patents Act 1988

This book has been typeset in Poliphilus
Printed in China

British Library Cataloguing in Publication Data:
a catalogue record for this book is available from the British Library

ISBN 978-1-4063-5161-3

www.walker.co.uk

Willy's Stories

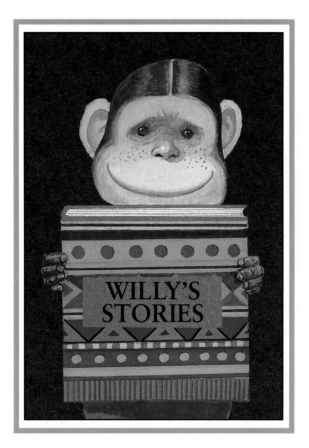

ANTHONY BROWNE

WALKER BOOKS

AND SUBSIDIARIES

LONDON · BOSTON · SYDNEY · AUCKLAND

VERY TIME I walk through these doors something incredible happens. I go on AMAZING adventures.

Come with me and I'll show you…

NE DAY I went through the doors and found I was shipwrecked with the Captain's dog on a desert island. I could see no one else there, and apart from a friendly parrot I was all alone. I walked by the sea looking for signs of life but I never saw anything.

Then, one day – I knew it was a Friday, as I had been marking the days on a calendar – I saw a FOOTPRINT IN THE SAND!

I froze as if I'd seen a ghost. I looked around, up and down the beach. I listened but I could see nothing and hear nothing. I checked to see if I had imagined the footprint (I sometimes do imagine things) but there it was – the exact shape of a foot, in the sand.

But I was sure; there was no one else on the island. I was STUNNED!

Whose footprint do YOU think it was?

 NOTHER TIME, when I went through the doors, I found I was a sailor on board a ship, looking for treasure. We had a map and the treasure was supposed to be hidden on an island. I was hungry and climbed into an apple barrel (yes, that's right – to get an apple).

As I hid inside the barrel I heard a sailor called Long John Silver whispering to some of his shipmates, telling them that as soon as the treasure had been found they would kill the Captain and the officers and keep the treasure for themselves.

Then he told one of the crew to get him an apple from the barrel. You can imagine how TERRIFIED I was! I wanted to jump out of the barrel and RUN, but I was too scared. I heard the sailor walk towards the barrel, and…

What do you think happened then?

ANOTHER DAY I went through the doors and into the countryside. I needed to cross a stream but I had my best clothes on and didn't want to get them wet. Then I saw a jolly-looking priest tucking into a pie, so I asked him if he would carry me over the water.

"WHAT?" he bellowed. "A pathetic little WIMP like you dares to ask ME, Friar Tuck, to carry YOU across?"

He paused, then his anger seemed to pass and his little eyes twinkled. "But why not?" he said. "Surely I can be merry too. I could help you, even though you are such a miserable creature."

The Friar tucked up his robe and bent down. "I think," he said with a smile, "your sword will get wet. Let me put it under my arm next to mine." I climbed on his back and Friar Tuck stepped into the water and waded forwards while I clung on for dear life. I did not want to fall into the water. When he reached the middle of the stream, where the water was deepest, he stopped, and began to laugh. I felt myself begin to slip.

Can you guess what happened next?

ONE TIME I went through the doors and found myself on a road where I met an old woman.

"Good evening, dearie," she said. "You look like a brave little soldier. I need some help. You see this tree here?"

"Y-yes," I said.

"This tree is hollow. If you climb up to the top, you'll see a hole down the trunk."

"What do I have to DO down in the tree?" I asked.

"If you look down the hole, you'll see a box at the bottom. It's called a tinderbox and my grandmother left it there especially for me. I want it, I REALLY want it. If I tie a rope round you, you'll be able to slide down to the bottom, pick up the box and I'll pull you back up when you call." I wanted to help her so I climbed to the top of the tree and looked down the dark hole inside. It was VERY deep and VERY dark.

"I – I don't think I can do it," I said.

"If you get me the tinderbox, I'll give you a lot of money," she shouted. "You'll be RICH!"

I didn't know what to do.

If you had been me, what would YOU have done?

 WENT through the doors one day and was on a pirate ship, face to face with a terrible pirate — CAPTAIN HOOK! For a long time we just stared at each other. Then Hook cleared his throat and said, "So, you horrible little man, PREPARE TO MEET YOUR END!"

He lunged at me with his sword. I jumped aside and a terrible fight began. We fought with our swords all over the ship. Then Hook came at me with his great iron hook, swinging both it and his sword together. Every sweep would have cut me in half but I dodged him, dancing around as if blown about by the wind.

At last we came to a stop, exhausted, and Hook looked at me with a strange expression. "Who and what ARE you?" he cried, exasperated.

"I'm YOUTH, I'm JOY," I answered. "I'm THE BOY WHO WON'T GROW UP!"

It was all nonsense of course, but something very strange happened next…

What do you think it was?

NE TIME I went through the doors and (I know it sounds crazy) I felt myself falling down a dark, deep hole – a rabbit hole. It was so deep that I had time to look around as I fell. The walls were covered with shelves full of curious objects and I grabbed at one as I tumbled down. "After a fall like this," I said to myself, "I'll never worry about falling down stairs again."

Down, down, down I went. Would this fall never end? Suddenly, with a WHOOSH! and a THUMP! I landed on a heap of dry leaves, but I wasn't hurt and jumped to my feet.

It was dark. As my eyes got used to the dim light I saw a figure with big ears hurrying down a long passage and turning a corner. I could swear it was a white rabbit, it looked at a pocket watch and then hurried on. I ran after it, around the corner, and THEN...

What do you think I saw?

**T**HE NEXT time when I went through the doors I found myself in a small grey room. There was a smelly little dog and through the window the sky was very dark. The wind WAILED and WHISTLED, the dog trumped and crept under the bed.

All of a sudden the room shook SO hard that I fell over. I felt the whole building WHIRLING about as it started to rise up in the air. The wind HOWLED horribly, but after a while I began to feel as if I was being rocked gently, like a baby in a cradle, and in spite of the swaying of the house and the wailing of the wind I closed my eyes and fell asleep.

I was woken by a huge BUMP as the house landed on the ground. It wasn't dark any more and bright sunshine flooded through the window. I looked out, and saw a yellow brick road stretching miles ahead. Walking along it, coming towards me, were some of the STRANGEST little people I'd ever seen.

Don't you want to find out who they were?

NOTHER TIME I went through the doors and found myself in a forest. I heard a voice singing BEAUTIFULLY in the distance and walked towards it. What creature could make such a lovely sound? I came to a tower and walked around it looking for a door – but there wasn't one. How peculiar! I saw a glistening rope, that looked as if it were made from golden hair, hanging down from the top of the tower. If that's the only way to get in, I thought, I'll climb up it.

I was desperate to see who was singing, so I started to climb the silky rope. At first it was quite easy, but when I looked down to see how far I'd come I was frightened. It was a VERY long way down! What if I were to fall?

Then the beautiful voice began again. I just HAD to find out who it was, so I carried on climbing. Higher and higher I went, full of doubts and worries. What was this silken rope? What if it were a TRAP, with a horrible WITCH at the top? I HAD to go on; I HAD to see who was there…

And when I got to the top, what do you think I found?

NE AFTERNOON I went through the doors and into a Wild Wood. It was both scary and exciting. Twigs crackled under my feet and fallen branches tripped me up.

Then the FACES appeared! I saw a strange little one looking at me from a hole. Quickly it vanished. I began to hurry, but another face appeared, and then another. I wished my friends Mr Toad and Ratty were with me. Then the WHISTLING began, faint at first, and far behind me. I went faster and heard the whistling again, this time ahead of me. Night was closing in. What could I do? Then the PATTERING started. It had a regular, sinister rhythm, like the PAT-PAT-PAT of little feet. But was it in front or behind me?

The sounds grew LOUDER and LOUDER and the whole wood now seemed to be running, chasing, hunting, closing in – on me?

I began to run, and saw a hollow tree to hide in. I crawled inside, panting and trembling with fear, listening to the noises outside. I knew I'd found that awful thing I had been told about – the TERROR OF THE WILD WOOD.

Was I in danger? WHAT do you think was chasing me?

AST WEEK I went through the doors and found myself swimming in a calm sea, when an ENORMOUS sea monster suddenly rose up in the water and made straight for me! Terrified, I swam as fast as I could, but it came nearer and nearer. I tried to dodge, to get out of its way, as I felt the great, gulping jaws SUCKING me towards it. Of course, I was too slow. The monstrous creature swallowed me greedily and I was swept into its stomach. I lay there, unconscious.

When I came round, I had no idea where I was. It was pitch black and there was no sound at all. I tried to be brave, but I was too frightened.

"H-E-L-P me," I cried, feebly. "Will someone P-L-E-A-S-E come and R-E-S-C-U-E me?" But no one did.

I had to help myself. In the distance I saw a dim light and followed my nose towards it. I walked and walked through the creature's body, until at long last I reached the light and saw the strangest thing.

WHAT DO YOU THINK IT WAS and WHO do you think I found? (You'll never guess, not in a million years . . .)

NEXT TIME, why don't you come with me on my travels, or better still, why not go on some of your own?

I can't wait for MY new adventure …

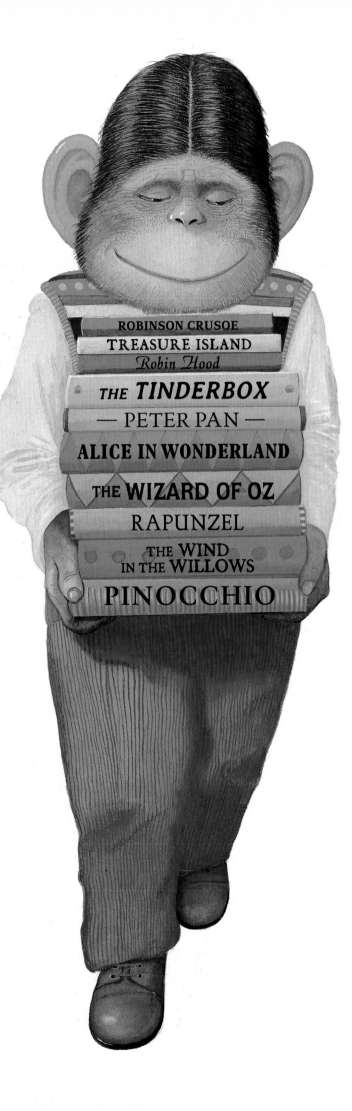

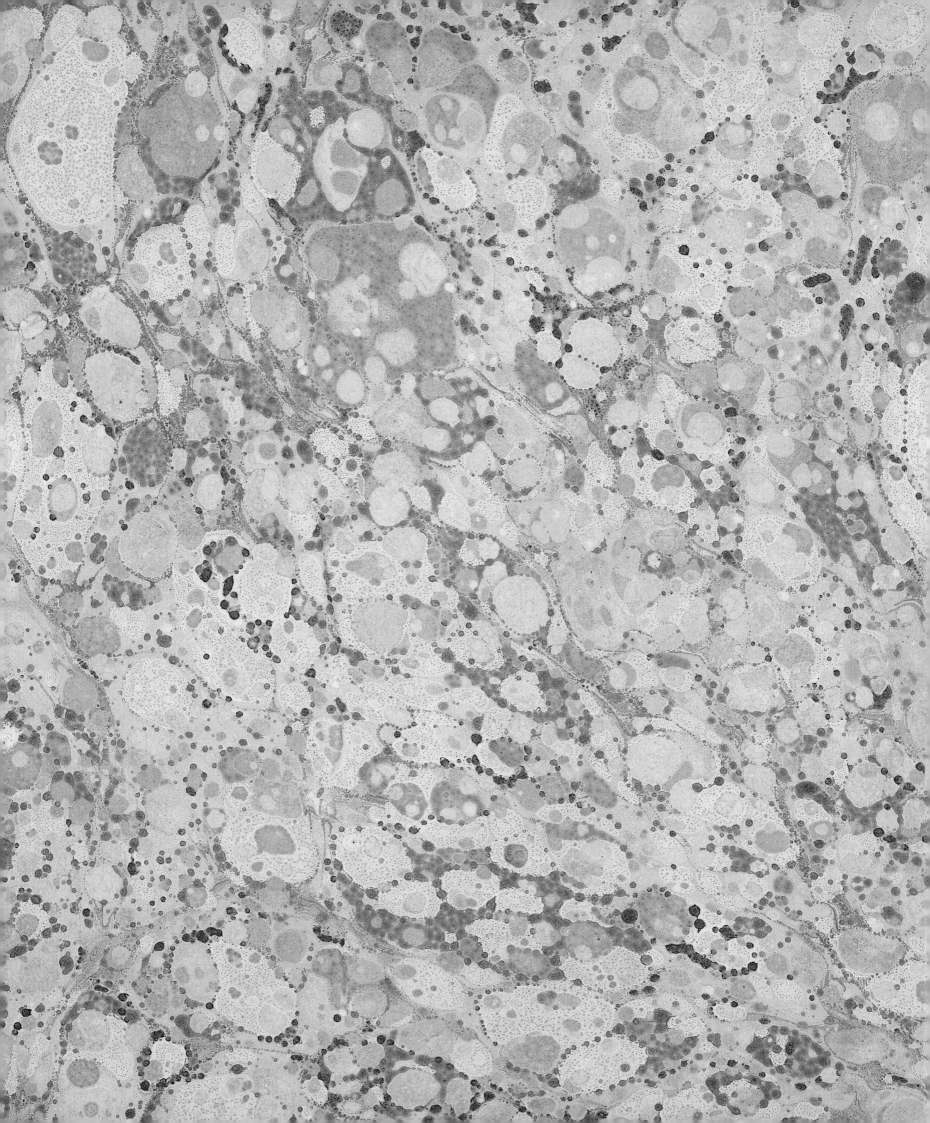